The Woman Pirate

The Woman Pirate

Thomas Wray McKee Jr.

ISBN: 978-1-6653-0532-7 - Paperback
eISBN: 978-1-6653-0533-4 - eBook

These ISBNs are the property of BookLogix for the express purpose of sales and distribution of this title. The content of this book is the property of the copyright holder only. BookLogix does not hold any ownership of the content of this book and is not liable in any way for the materials contained within. The views and opinions expressed in this book are the property of the Author/Copyright holder, and do not necessarily reflect those of BookLogix.

⊗This paper meets the requirements of ANSI/NISO Z39.48-1992 (Permanence of Paper)

0 3 2 6 2 4

Photos by Thomas Wray McKee Jr.
Author photo by Jeff Philips

*Dedicated to my little brother, Billy,
and my sister, Mary Ellen.*

Introduction

My name is Thomas Wray McKee Jr., born September 29, 1983, in Savannah, Georgia. I grew up in Savannah, and when I was a kid, I attended a day camp called Coastal Ecology Camp. When I got into high school, I worked three summers as a counselor at this camp.

Every Thursday we would have a new batch of kids and we would arrive at my school at five in the morning, and drive about an hour south down the interstate to McIntosh County. We would catch the ferry to Sapelo Island and spend the day there. Sapelo is one of Georgia's barrier islands, which means it borders the Atlantic Ocean. It is a nature preserve owned by the US government.

There is a small African American community who are allowed to live, hunt, and fish on the island. They are descendants of the slaves that used to work the island. They have a small general store in their community. They speak the Creole dialect Gullah, which is an offshoot of English. They make their living weaving cast nets and things of this sort. They call their community Hog Hammock.

The University of Georgia has a marine lab on the corner of the island. At one point, R. J. Reynolds, the tobacco tycoon, owned the island and built a mansion in the center. These days, with a group of about ten or eleven people, this mansion can be rented. There are dirt and paved roads which crisscross the island, and it is incredibly beautiful.

When I was in my mid- to late-twenties, I spent a night on Sapelo and brought along a camera. I wrote my pirate story around the same time. I tried to use stream of consciousness, and I tried to make it easy to read. At the time, I was under the impression that "stream of consciousness" referred to writing whatever was on your mind. I found out later that it involved putting the character's, or characters', thoughts on paper. I did sit down and write what was on my mind, and I decided not to change the story after I wrote it except to make it grammatically correct and historically accurate. I wrote it in two days.

Over the years I did a little research and revised it. I just completed it this morning, and the date today is November 12, 2020. In the following pages you will see the pictures I took when I spent the night on the island.

Sapelo Island Post Office

Graveyard

Sapelo Island Lighthouse

Sapelo Island Range Front Lighthouse

Broken Sand Dollars on Front Beach

View of Atlantic Ocean over Front Beach with Tidal Pool

Sand Dunes of Front Beach

Stairs onto Front Beach

View to the North Looking Down Front Beach

View to the South Looking Down Front Beach

Stairs Leading Down to Front Beach

View to the South Looking Down Front Beach

Historic Reynolds Mansion

Sapelo Island Cultural and Revitalization Society

The University of Georgia Marine Institute

Church

Another View of Reynolds mansion

Live Oak Trees with Spanish Moss

Gazebo

Author Thomas Wray McKee Jr.

Ferry at Dock

Live Oak Trees with Spanish Moss

Sign for Ferry

The Woman Pirate

J immy was a young man, just turned eighteen. The year was 1778; Jamaica was the place. Being under British rule at the time, the island was bustling with excitement. But Jimmy was one of the delinquents. He had struggled through most of his life.

When he became a man, his father found him a job on a fishing boat on the coast. Jimmy had grown up on the ocean but never spent much time on the water. He was not too excited about the idea of fishing for a living, but being morally strong, he listened to his father. Jimmy was an only child, and his parents fit nicely in the middle of the middle class. Growing up, he never had much, but there was always food on the table, and his parents' relationship seemed strong. Nonetheless, the month of October found him setting sail on a fishing boat. Jimmy made the fifth member in a crew of five: one captain and four deckhands. Jimmy was far and away the youngest member of the crew.

Jimmy learned the ropes of the boat fast and took to something for the first time in his life. Unfortunately, he was not treated too well by the others in the crew, but by the time a week passed, he had learned to deal with it.

There was one mate—Bill was his name—who had taken to Jimmy since day one. But he was careful not to show it so as not to anger the other members of the crew, but Jimmy had noticed. When the crew got to complaining about their lifestyle and how, really, they would be content with anything other than fishing, Bill kept his mouth shut. Jimmy, on the other hand, found himself pretty content on the water. When the captain on the first day was explaining to Jimmy the ways of the boat, he told him that seven days on the water was standard, then it was back to the mainland to unload the catch.

On the seventh day, Jimmy was lounging on the deck when something on the horizon caught his eye. He was not sure what it was, but assumed it was another fishing boat. From what he could tell, it was headed in their direction. He went below to get the rusty spyglass to get a better look. He put the glass to his eye and nearly dropped it in fear. The white skull and crossbones silhouetted by black, flying high, was unmistakable. And he was right—it was headed right for them. He ran to tell the rest of the crew, and found himself bursting with anger when they seemed excited about getting to know some pirates, Bill included. Jimmy searched for a weapon to defend himself, but all he could come up with was an old mop handle.

About five minutes passed, and the pirate ship was alongside Jimmy's boat. Jimmy spat on the deck when he saw his captain raising a white napkin in a sign of surrender. Jimmy found himself trembling with fear as a plank slid across from the pirate deck to his boat. Still gripping his mop handle tight, he watched in fear as a beautiful woman, clothed in pirate attire, holding in her a hand a gun, walked across the plank and boarded Jimmy's boat. She made her way to Jimmy's captain, the click-clacks of her boots on the deck echoing in Jimmy's ear.

"Good decision," she said as she took the white napkin and placed it in her pocket. "What do you think, boys?" she said.

A loud cheer came from the men slowly appearing at the rail of the pirate ship.

She caught Jimmy's eye, pointed the gun, and said, "Drop it, son."

Jimmy lost consciousness and fell to the deck.

Jimmy woke on the deck of the pirate ship in time to watch the fishing boat he had grown fond of disappear beneath the waves. As he slowly regained consciousness, Jimmy looked on in disgust at the other members of his crew mixing and min-gling with the pirates. He saw Bill approaching.

"How are you feeling, son?" said Bill.

"I'm all right, I guess," said Jimmy. "Can I ask you a question?"

"Shoot," said Bill.

"Why are y'all bowing to these thieves?"

"So, we're thieves, are we?" said a voice from behind Jimmy. Jimmy spun around to see one of the pirates looking him dead in the eye with a toothless grin, fingering his knife.

In desperation, Jimmy said, "I didn't mean it."

"Hey, Bobby-do-right here thinks we're thieves," said the pirate. "Wish you had that broom handle, don't you?"

"Back off!" said a loud woman's voice.

"Sorry, Cap," said the pirate, "just breaking in the newbies."

"Walk with me for a second," said the captain to Jimmy. Feeling like he had no choice, Jimmy am-bled after the captain. He followed her to the back of the boat, where she stopped.

She turned to Jimmy and said, "Not too excited about becoming a pirate, huh?"

"Not really," Jimmy said.

"Well, the way I see it, you have two choices: we can throw you overboard and let you swim back to Jamaica, or you can join us and sail to America."

"A-America!" Jimmy stammered.

"That's where we're headed."

"Well, seeing as we're a good two weeks' swim from Jamaica, I guess I have no choice," said Jimmy sarcastically.

The captain chuckled. "I guess not."

"Where in America?" Jimmy asked.

"We're bound for Savannah—that's where I plan on retiring."

"What about the revolution?" said Jimmy.

"Not sure what you're talking about," said the captain.

"You know, the war over the colonies?" said Jimmy.

"Tell me more."

"Well, I guess you haven't heard. It's all anyone

talks about on the mainland. The colonies in America have declared independence and are fighting the king's army. The war's been going on for over a year now. England is pretty confident they'll squash it, but so far, the colonies are holding their own."

The captain appeared to think for a second, and said, "It's decided. We'll fight with the colonies."

"What!" said Jimmy. "I thought you were planning on retiring?"

"Listen, kid, the British government and I go way back. I'll take any chance I can to teach them their lesson."

"With all due respect, you're a pirate. I don't think you're in much of a place to teach anybody a lesson."

"Noted," said the captain. "I'd like to talk to you some more. Come knock on my door in half an hour." She turned and left Jimmy, the click-clacks of her boots once more echoing in his ears.

Jimmy wandered the deck, looking for Bill. He

found him leaning on the rail on the side of the ship, gazing at the open water.

"We're headed for America," said Jimmy.

"Don't much matter to me, the question you asked me earlier."

"Why?"

"Son, you have to understand, you have got your whole life ahead of you. The rest of us—well, the sun is setting. Although us fisherman make it in this life, it is not ideal. Joining a pirate crew— well, at least it's exciting."

"But still, you're breaking the law, risking your life!"

"Yes, that is true, and to be honest, it makes me hesitate, but in the end, it beats fishing the life out of yourself. Maybe one day you'll understand."

"I guess so," said Jimmy.

"While you're stuck on this ship, try to make the best of it."

"Good advice," said Jimmy.

Jimmy waited out the rest of his half hour, star-ing out over the Caribbean, chatting with Bill.

After thirty minutes had passed, he wandered over to the captain's quarters and rapped on the door.

"Come in," she said. He opened the door and found her seated at a desk, her long blonde hair hanging over her shoulders.

"Grab a seat," she said.

Jimmy pulled a stool off the wall.

The captain was fingering a small porcelain dish. She removed the lid and handed it to Jimmy. "You know what that is?"

Jimmy looked at the black tar inside the dish.

"Smell it," she said.

He did so, and said, "Opium."

"Will you smoke with me?" she said.

"Sure," said Jimmy. Jimmy had smoked plenty before for his age, so it was nothing new to him.

The captain produced a glass pipe with two snakes wrapping around it. She packed the pipe and lit it with a match. She inhaled and handed it to Jimmy, who did the same. After the tar in the pipe was all burned, the captain broke the silence.

"So, what's a young man like you doing on a fishing boat?"

"Well," Jimmy said, his tongue loosening as the opium set in. "I couldn't quite cut it in the classroom, so my father found me this. I'll be honest with you: I was beginning to enjoy it until I met you."

The captain chuckled. "A noble profession to be sure. But wouldn't you like a little more excitement?"

"Yeah, sure, as long as a noose isn't waiting for me."

"Well, once we get to Savannah, that will change, especially with this revolution you talk about."

"Why piracy?" asked Jimmy. "You seem like a decent woman."

"A little bold of you, don't you think?" said the captain.

"Maybe," said Jimmy. "But I just cannot understand it. How can one's heart be that black?"

"I wasn't always this way. Believe it or not, I set

my course with noble intentions. Maybe I got lost somewhere along the way."

"Noble intentions! How is that possible?"

"Let me tell you a story. A story of a young woman growing up on the coast of England. My story," she said.

"I've got nothing but time," said Jimmy.

"Well, growing up, I loved the ocean, and I'll tell you, like you, I disdained pirates. I thought they turned something beautiful ugly. By the time I was your age, I was married to the most perfect of men. He was an officer in the East India company, ten years my elder. One day he was faced with a decision: one way, he would disobey orders, another, he would massacre an innocent village. He chose the former, and was hanged for it.

"My life was ruined, and a seed of hatred was planted in me. I turned to piracy as a way out. I have been at it for over twenty years now, and that seed has blossomed in the process. But I tell you what: meeting you has made me question a lot of things for the first time in those twenty years. I want to thank you for that. But a black heart? I wouldn't go that far."

Jimmy sat stunned by her story. "I'm sorry, I had no idea," he said quietly.

"That's all right," she said. "Now, are you with us, or against us?"

"I don't have much of a choice," said Jimmy.

"This may be the opium talking, but I want to give you something. It belonged to my husband." She reached in the drawer and pulled out a small knife.

Jimmy took it and unsheathed it. "It's beautiful," he said, admiring the precious stones in the handle.

By this time, the sun was setting.

"Now, I'd like you to get some sleep. We should arrive in Yatero in a little while. We will stock up on supplies for the journey."

Jimmy found a hammock on the deck and fell asleep.

When they arrived at Yatero, the captain was at the wheel, and all hands were on deck. Jimmy noticed that the skull and crossbones was not flying, and the crew, along with the captain, was dressed in street clothes.

The remainder of the day was spent readying the lifeboats and preparing the ship and crew to go ashore. Once the boat was safely anchored in the harbor, evening was falling.

Jimmy found a lifeboat, hunkered down, and sat stone still as it was rowed ashore. Once on land, the captain caught his shoulder and handed him a small bag. He opened it and counted twenty gold coins. The first chance he got, he slipped down an alley and lost everyone.

In the back of his mind, he knew there was no way he would ever make it back to Jamaica, and he felt a strange sadness deep inside his bones. He slipped into the first pub he could find, sat down on a barstool, and proceeded to drown his sorrows.

He handed the bartender a gold coin and asked for two bottles of rum. The bartender examined the coin carefully and accepted Jimmy's offer. He disappeared for several minutes.

Jimmy looked around the room. It was dim, lit only by lamps and candles. There were tables and chairs and several barstools like the one he was seated on. The pub was filled to about a third of its capacity, split about halfway male and female, mostly middle-aged. From the looks of it, he was the youngest in the room, but the bartender had not bothered with his age, so Jimmy shrugged it off.

After several minutes passed, the bartender returned with two bottles of rum and a glass and handed them to Jimmy. Jimmy thanked him, took his bottles and glass, and retired to a lone table in the corner.

His mind began to drift to the future as he unscrewed the cap. What would he do with the rest of his life? He certainly had not planned on becoming a pirate when he got older. He remembered being a kid and dreaming of working with his father, maybe taking a wife and raising a family, growing old and living out his days in a nice house with a little garden. But here he was, a fugitive in a corner, drinking rum in a strange bar. As young as he was, even he had to admit life does not always work out as planned.

He shook it off and poured a glass. Nineteen gold coins left. He took a sip and felt a little burn as it went down. Thirty minutes later found him drunk.

The captain watched Jimmy walk away. She shook her head and chuckled, wondering if she would ever see him again. She told herself he would be all right; at least he had twenty gold pieces. As he disappeared, she went along her way. She began to dispatch the crew, sending them this way and that with money and bags to get what they would need for their journey to Savannah. She was hoping they could get what they needed to make it in one shot. If not, they would have to make an emergency stop in Florida before they reached their destination. Once everyone had gone on their way, the captain decided to take a walk around town.

Jimmy, feeling the effects of the rum, caught the eye of a young lady across the room. She was no more than twenty-five, and she was what you might call a looker. Already under the influence, Jimmy grinned and tipped his hat. As he saw her smile, he filled his glass, took a sip, and stood up. He slowly approached her table.

She was sitting by herself, sipping rum. He introduced himself politely and sat down. She told him her name was Anne.

As Jimmy was about to open his mouth again, he heard a loud voice behind him say belligerently, "Anne."

Jimmy turned his head to see a large drunken man stumbling toward him with a knife. In a drunken daze, Jimmy stood and turned. His hand slid to the knife the captain had given him that hung at his waist.

As the man approached, Jimmy readied himself. Before he had time to think, the man lunged forward, knife in hand. Jimmy sidestepped, and the man swung his arm left and right. In a panic, Jimmy moved behind him and, in one drunken move, slit his throat.

The man fell to the floor and bled out.

The bar went silent.

Anne screamed.

Jimmy ran out the door, into the street, and slipped into the darkness.

Once out of sight, he sheathed his bloody knife and slipped down a back alley. By this point, he was seeing double. He checked his pocket to make sure he still had his nineteen gold coins. Sure enough, he did. His mind was racing. He knew he must find the captain and get back to the boat. Unfortunately, he was stone drunk and had no idea where he was.

Back at the bar, Anne was bent over the man lying on the ground in a pool of blood. Tears were running down her face. The man was her fiancé. She was a young woman, a basket weaver in the market. The man, a good deal older than her, had asked her to marry him no more than a month before.

The other customers were in shock at what they had just witnessed. Some were trying to console Anne; others had simply got up and left. The bartender knew it was his duty to notify the authorities. He was talking with two young men, who were sober enough for the errand.

The captain was walking down main street trying to decide what to do with herself. She was noticing the stores and the people. She decided to grab a drink. She slipped into a pub, sat down at a table, and ordered a drink. She let her eyes wander the room. Mostly young couples and drunks. She felt herself slipping into a strange depression as she watched the couples enjoying their meals together. She thought of Jimmy, and how she had turned an innocent young man onto piracy. She swore to herself that when the revolution he talked about was over, she would lay down her sword for good.

To cure her mood, she downed her drink and ordered another. She noticed a drunken boy eyeing her from across the room. She kept her seat. After about five minutes and few more drinks, he approached her. He sat down and bought her a drink.

The crew spent the night purchasing and gathering the things they would need for their journey. They worked into the night, traveling from the town to the boat until everything was ready. By morning, everything was prepared.

The captain had spent the night with the young man she had met at the bar, and slipped out before he woke. She arrived back at the boat to find things in order as the sun was rising. Only Jimmy was missing.

There was a pirate in the crew named Henry who had worked into the night, gathering things for the voyage. Around midnight, he was pushing a cart down the street when he saw the local authorities hauling Jimmy down the street in handcuffs. When the captain arrived back at the boat in the morning, Henry approached her.

"Cap."

"Yes, Henry."

"You know the young kid we picked up from the fishing boat?"

"You mean Jimmy?"

"Yeah, I guess he's the one."

"What of him?"

"Well, last night I saw the authorities hauling him off in cuffs. What should we do?"

The captain paused. "We shall not leave him behind."

"Didn't think so," said Henry.

"Is everything ready for the journey?" asked the captain.

"Far as I know," said Henry.

"Well, all that's left to do is spring young Jimmy from the jailhouse."

Jimmy woke from a blackout to find himself sitting in a jail cell. The last thing he could remember was a man coming at him with a knife. The charges against him were murder in the first degree. The cell was damp and dirty, he was alone, and he had never felt more alone in his whole life. He did not know what the future held.

The fact of the matter was he had committed no crime. Perhaps he should have stayed out of the bar in the first place. Perhaps he was too young to be drinking. Perhaps he should have never approached a woman. But his crime was self-defense. But being a stranger in town, all alone, as young as he was, and a pirate nonetheless, he had no way to defend himself. And to make matters worse, the sun was rising. His heart sank as low as it could go when he realized that the captain and crew were probably setting sail. He hung his head and cried.

Back on the boat, the captain gathered five crewmembers—Henry was one of them, and Bill volunteered for the task. They armed themselves with guns and knives. They entered the captain's chambers and proceeded to draw up a plan to rescue their young shipmate.

Jimmy sat alone in his jail cell. As his tears dried, he began to wonder how he had gotten himself into this mess. He told himself he had not done anything wrong, but he could not help feeling guilty. He missed his home; he knew that he would probably never see it again. He tried to be a man and look to the future. Perhaps he would survive this mess and make it to Savannah. Perhaps, once there, he could build a life for himself. But despite trying, he could not see the light. Maybe he deserved it, he told himself. Maybe he simply was not worthy. He surrendered.

Once the plan was drawn up and everything was in order, the captain, Bill, Henry, and the other three pirates climbed into a lifeboat dressed in street clothes, armed with their weapons, and rowed ashore. The jailhouse that held Jimmy was small and not heavily guarded. The six of them were not entirely sure what they were up against, but Henry knew where to take them.

They followed Henry to the end of town—this is where the jailhouse sat. It was a small building, containing three cells. Jimmy's cell had a window opening to the outside in the back. Bill was sent there; he was able to arrive undetected. There was one way in and one way out: one door.

Inside was a lone room surrounded by the three cells. On the side of the room was a desk. At the desk sat a guard; he was armed and held the keys. There were others who came and went, but there was no way for the captain and crew to know the schedule, so they had to take their chances.

Once the captain and her small crew had taken in the scene, they finalized their plan, and sent Bill 'round to Jimmy's window.

Jimmy's head was hanging low when he heard Bill's voice whisper, "Jimmy, ya in there?"

Jimmy nearly jumped in excitement, but he was careful to keep his voice low and not move a muscle. "Yeah, I'm in here, Bill. Boy, am I glad to hear your voice."

"We're comin' for you. Just hold tight," Bill said.

Just then, the door opened, and the captain casually walked in, drew her gun, pointed it at the guard, and said, "Give me the key to that kid's cell," and pointed at Jimmy. Henry and the others were outside, guarding the door and the surrounding area with caution. The guard hesitated. The captain cocked her gun and said sternly, "Now, or you die."

The guard handed her the key. She walked over to the cell, keeping an eye on the guard and the gun pointed at him.

Jimmy stood and did not say a word. He felt a chill in his body. The Captain turned the key and opened the door. They walked out together, the captain all the while staring the guard in the eye with her gun pointed at him.

Once outside, Bill joined them. Jimmy, the captain, Bill, Henry, and the other three crewmembers turned the corner, disappeared, and headed back to the ship.

When Anne found out who the killer in the bar was, she rushed home to tell her younger sister, Carla. Carla was full grown and was three years her younger. She also was a basket weaver in the local market.

Anne and Carla had lost their parents at a young age and, with the loss of Anne's fiancé, were all alone in the world. They quickly made up their minds to pack what little belongings they had and head to the docks.

The small rescue party made their way back to the docks as quickly as they could, once they had Jimmy in tow.

Back at the boat, the pirates were readying the relatively small pirate ship for the captain and the rescue party to return. They were lining the rails of the ship, fully armed. They had lowered a rope ladder down the side of the ship.

Anne and Carla arrived at the docks early in the morning. Under cover of darkness, they were able to slip into a small rowboat unnoticed, row to the pirate ship, climb aboard, and slip below deck unnoticed. They had each armed themselves with a gun for the journey.

The harbor was silent as the sun rose. The pirates on the deck waited anxiously for the captain's return. The crew that had remained on the ship had their backs to the open water and were staring across the harbor toward the town. As dawn broke and the world began to light up for another day, Anne and Carla drew their guns and climbed the stairs toward the deck as quietly as they could.

Anne and Carla were able to arrive on deck without any of the pirates noticing. They found the crew silently staring across the harbor with their backs to Anne and Carla. Anne cocked her gun and pointed at the crew. The pirates heard the gun cock. One of the crew toward the far end of the line was able to slip behind Anne and Carla without them noticing.

Anne said, "One of you pirates murdered my fiancé. I'm here to seek my revenge."

The pirate who had slipped behind Anne and Carla—Trip was his name—drew his knife and put it to Carla's throat.

Trip had had a talk with Henry before the rescue party had been assembled. He said, "The boy's name is Jimmy. He's one of us, and until our captain returns with him and we find out what really happened, you will hand over your guns, or I will slit this young lady's throat."

Anne and Carla did as they were told. One of the crew fetched a rope, and the pirates tied Anne and Carla to the mast. Several of the pirates volunteered to watch them, and the rest of the crew returned to the rail to await the captain's return.

Once Jimmy had escaped, the man at the jail alerted the rest of the town's authorities, and they quickly began to search for the boy.

They caught the pirates at the harbor as they were rowing toward the ship. The guard from the jail identified Jimmy, and the authorities opened fire. The pirates lining the rail of the ship returned fire. The rescue party safely made it to the ship and began climbing the rope ladder. Bill was shot in the leg as he was climbing the ladder, but with Jimmy's help, he was able to make it aboard.

The ship hastily set sail and got away.

Once the boat made open water, the captain addressed the two girls tied to the mast.

Jimmy recognized Anne, and Anne recognized Jimmy. Anne began scolding Jimmy, calling him a murderer. Jimmy was hurt, and he apologized to her, but explained that his crime was self-defense.

Anne went quiet and appeared to think. After a while, she opened her mouth. She accepted Jimmy's apology and explained to the captain her and Carla's situation. The captain offered to bring them safely to Savannah in return for joining their crew. Anne and Carla discussed their situation in their native language and accepted the captain's offer.

Peace was made, Anne and Carla were untied, and the captain set her course for Sapelo Island. For the remainder of the journey, Anne mourned the loss of her fiancé.

Sailing up the coast of Florida, the pirates intercepted a British party boat. Aboard, they found a chest containing plans to move one of the king's treasures up the coast. The pirates successfully stole the treasure and got away.

One morning on the way to Sapelo, Jimmy was fishing, and he got one. He fought it all day, and as night was falling, with his hands blistered and bloody, and the help of the crew, he hauled aboard a full-grown blue marlin. The crew ate good that night, and Jimmy got many a pat on the back.

When the pirates made Sapelo, they anchored the boat off the beach, and rowed into the dunes with their treasure.

The captain announced that those that wished to forgo the war would be given their share of the booty and sent on their way. Most of the crew decided to do this; Anne and Carla were among them. Jimmy and Bill decided to stay behind and fight with the captain. Those that decided to remain behind buried what remained of the treasure and sailed to the mouth of the Savannah River.

They sailed up the river to River Street, tied the boat to the dock, and made their way through a tunnel under the street into a local tavern.

The captain had cut her hair and dressed like a man. Inside the tavern, there was a man taking names for the American militia. The captain, Jimmy, Bill, and the remainder of the crew gave their names.

They were stationed on the Isle of Hope, guarding the Moon River. A month went by, and they saw no action. One day, they saw the British approaching. A bloody battle ensued, and after the battle, the British were on the run. Jimmy and Bill were among the survivors. They quickly found each other and searched for the rest of the crew. They found the captain lying on the ground, covered in blood, clutching the treasure map in her hands. She handed it to Jimmy, who placed it in his pocket as carefully as he could. The rest of the crew was dead. The captain was able to walk, and with Jimmy and Bill's help, she made it to a local inn.

Jimmy sat with the captain and prayed while Bill rushed out to find a doctor. He shortly returned with one. The doctor examined the captain and informed Bill and Jimmy that with proper rest she would pull through. They breathed a sigh of relief.

To be continued . . .

Acknowledgments

I would like to thank my little brother, Billy, for providing me with some historical information, and Lisa Breitberg, who accompanied me to Sapelo when I took the pictures.

About the Author

Thomas Wray McKee Jr. was born and raised in Savannah, Georgia. For high school, he attended Savannah Country Day School. After high school, he attended Duke University.